CALLING
OUTER SPACE

Jean Nugent

Illustrations by Robert Roper

S0-BAT-701

SCHOLASTIC INC.
New York Toronto London Auckland Sydney Tokyo

To Katy B.,
whose laughter and hearty "you can do it"
got me through this time.
To Pat, Tim, Bill, and Dave,
who said the same thing once before.

No part of this publication may be reproduced in whole
or in part, or stored in a retrieval system, or transmit-
ted in any form or by any means, electronic, mechan-
ical, photocopying, recording, or otherwise, without
written permission of the publisher. For information
regarding permission, write to Scholastic Inc., 730
Broadway, New York, NY 10003.

ISBN 0-590-33236-8

Copyright © 1985 by Jean Nugent. All rights reserved.
Published by Scholastic Inc. by arrangement with
Parachute Press, Inc.

12 11 10 9 8 7 6 5 4 3 2   5 6 7 8 9/8 0/9

Printed in the U.S.A.   01

BEWARE!!!
DO NOT READ THIS BOOK FROM BEGINNING TO END

You are about to embark on a perilous journey into the uncharted vastness of outer space. The fate of Earth depends upon the decisions you make. So read the directions at the bottom of each page carefully. Decide which choice is the best, and then boldly follow your instincts to the correct page. The slightest mistake will mean danger, galactic destruction . . . or instant death.

But don't worry. If you are clever, courageous, or just plain lucky, you will accomplish your mission and return to the sunny safety of Earth once again.

Prepare to beam into an extra-terrestrial adventure you won't soon forget! You'll be shocked to find how many answers you receive when you find yourself calling outer space!

Go on to PAGE 2.

"Win the science fair? YOU?" Fred's snickering words replay in your mind. Fred's computer club had a good laugh at your expense. Of course you *were* bragging that your radio telescope would take the blue ribbon.

Maybe it would have been better if you had skipped that part about contacting extra-terrestrials. "ET phone home?" Fred squeaked.

Your face reddens again at the memory of Fred's wisecracks. You lean out your bedroom window and yank in the parabolic scanner cables dangling from the roof. Angrily you screw down the antenna hookups to your crystal radio receiver and transmitter. Let them laugh, you think.

Get more data on PAGE 3.

Soon the dish-shaped antenna is activated. It's time. Hands trembling, you transmit the message: CALLING OUTER SPACE. CALLING OUTER SPACE. The signal repeats automatically as you lock keys into place. In one hour, the receiver and recorder will automatically switch on to see—you shiver at the thought—if anyone answers.

In bed, hours later, you hear the receiver click off and on two times. Maybe it's nothing but . . . you have to check.

Not wanting to wake your parents, you tiptoe to the equipment, rewind the recording tape, and push REPLAY. Crackling sounds blast your eardrums and you jump to reduce the volume. You strain to listen through the static. Suddenly you hear something—faint pulsing throbs. Slowly the sound becomes clearer. *Thump, thump, thump.* Pause. *Thump, thump.* Could this be outer space returning your call?!

Shaking, you grab a pencil and scribble as the pulses repeat. Are they dots and dashes like your signal? No. Three and two must indicate short-wave radio frequencies! But which should you tune into first?

Three kilohertz? Go to PAGE 12.
Two kilohertz? Go to PAGE 27.
If you think it's just static, go back to bed on PAGE 19.

Fred! With luck, Finder might *really* take him to Zeta 12. Of course Fred won't be suitable either, but he'll never make fun of you again! If Finder thinks *you* are too much trouble, wait until he gets a load of Fred!

Back in the main lounge, Finder reactivates the molecular scrambler and watches while the energy cycle maximizes. His cool eyes appraise you and he wrings his hands. "I *thought* you were a qualified EC! Reasonably intelligent. Curious . . ." His voice drones.

You chuckle, imagining Fred meeting Finder. Your chuckles become laughter.

Finder's voice snaps you out of it. "However, extra-celestials *must* be emotionally stable."

Now's the time to mention Fred. "Well, I guess you found my weakness," you sigh. "But so your trip won't be wasted, let me make a suggestion."

Minutes later the scrambler delivers you and Finder to your backyard. You draw Finder a map to Fred's house and wave good-bye. As soon as you close the front door, you start to laugh once more. You can't help it.

THE END

Finder only cares about getting you to the Search Council, you're sure. After that . . . well, you won't wait for after that!

You hold your breath and leap into the swirling colors, expecting your feet to find solid ground. They don't. Instead, your limbs plunge into banks of vapor. Both fearful and fascinated, you watch as your hands turn blue, your arms scarlet, and your legs a deep dark green.

Suddenly a generator hums and the air fills with the smell of bitter ozone. Then everything goes black.

Have you floated somewhere over the rainbow? Find out on PAGE 11.

Retrieving an overturned stool, you raise Marlin's feet. You are reaching for his pulse when the old man's eyes flutter open.

But before Marlin speaks, Lexor's crippled warship pitches, tossing you both down the sudden incline.

"I've got the escape craft!" you yell as Marlin tries to stagger to his feet. "C'mon . . . follow me!"

"No! *You* follow *me!*" Dragging himself along a handrail and out the hangar toward a small glowing console, you hear him add, "Get to the Macron Transporter Substation. It's our only chance! This ship is about to blow!"

Crawl or drag yourself to PAGE 79. But hurry!

You don't trust the macron beam. Choosing your spacecraft instead, you leap off the platform, hollering for Marlin to follow you to it. The ship lurches again and you tumble into the bay. When a control panel stops your somersaults, you look for Marlin in time to catch his horrified expression and hand reaching out to grab you. Then his image fades. The warship rumbles and you know you've made a mistake. Explosions rip through the ship. This is the end for you. . . .

But not the end of your fame. After Marlin reaches Earth, he tells your parents about your bravery and your fate. They miss you but invite Marlin to stay in your room. To earn a living, he sells stories describing your space battles with the evil Octedron knight. The stories are an instant success. Marlin becomes a famous science-fiction writer. Soon your name joins other fictional heroes like Luke Skywalker and Mr. Spock. They make a major motion picture of your life. It's titled *Calling Outer Space*.

THE END

Finally the whine stops and the ship stabilizes. Bree's smile signals the end of danger, and you force your fingers to release the armrests. Then ahead, you spot a wonderful sight. "I know *that* star! It's Polaris!" you shout, tracing the familiar pattern of the Little Dipper.

"And there is Earth." Bree indicates a blue-white speck shining in the distant sky.

Unfortunately, when Bree lands you discover that your Earth *has* changed . . . even more than you. Because of the space-storm, you arrive too late to issue your warning. Lexor has taken over.

Although it's difficult for your parents to let you go again, you and Bree leave to form the nucleus of an underground fighting force. You vow that with the blend of Koorian and Earth skills, somehow you'll defeat Lexor. No matter how long it takes!

THE END

You decide that your only chance is to make a break for the door. You race for the lighted opening and shove past the startled old man. The bright corridor blinds you after Lexor's dim control room, but you speed on sightlessly. In seconds the glare fades and you slow down. The only footsteps you hear are your own, echoing in empty passages. Is everyone asleep?

Halls branch left and right. Which way? You can't decide. Panic flares; then on a hunch you turn right.

Take the right passage to PAGE 32.

Incredibly, your eyes open again. You check to see if you're all there. Arms, legs, and feet are all attached in the usual way. But only after double-checking fingers and toes are you aware of being scrunched between piles of packing crates. Squinting, you read letters stamped on each box— SATURNIAN SHIPPERS: HAULING ANYTHING, ANYWHERE. Saturn! I'd sure like to see that, you think.

Peering around a column of containers, you look to the far end of the bustling warehouse. Rusty hover-cranes load more crates aboard a huge spacecraft marked SS1. Knots of helmeted men scurry up and down the craft's ramps shouting directions to one another. Overhead, the scene is lit by spotlights that cast hazy glints off a transparent dome.

You must be in a space station. That chamber must have transported you here, and you're not sure it's the best place to stay.

Look for a clue to your next move on PAGE 62.

Rotating the tuning knob toward a lighted "3" on the dial, you hear sounds. Faint at first, a flat voice utters something unintelligible. Your heart races. Every ten seconds it seems to repeat. Quickly you try timing the intervals between signals. Then static interferes with reception.

You push away from the set. Now you suspect the "voice" may be only space noise—natural impulses emitted from a planet or star.

You yawn. Some astronomer! Can't even recognize a *real* message! Give it up for tonight, you think. You also think, what if I miss something?

Too sleepy to decide, you pick up a penny.

Flip it. Heads, you force yourself to stay awake on PAGE 65.

Tails, you switch on the recorder, then go to bed. See what tomorrow brings on PAGE 71.

Fighting impatience, you drop the steering column and wait for Baramus to move. You're too new at this space-battle stuff to try anything alone.

Just then Baramus ignites his starboard engine and the flagship moves back. Split seconds later, Lexor fires energy beams that explode in the exact spot Baramus had been. Shock waves blow you and the squadron like puffballs, but you are unharmed, thanks to Baramus's move out of firing range.

Great Galaxy! Lexor was faking defeat, and you almost fell into his trap. Luckily, Baramus was warned by Marlin in time. You sigh, hoping that was Lexor's *last* trick.

A moment later, swarms of enemy wasp-fighters zoom in from nowhere. You can't believe it! The evil knight had more gunships hidden in space! Hypnotized by his force, you stare at black fighters that keep coming . . . and coming, until you lose count.

This adds up to big trouble on PAGE 77.

You'd rather get out of this on your own so you won't have to trust *aliens* like this fishy Bree character!

Before either Bree or the old man can react, you crouch and duck through an open hatch. Your confidence soars when you reach a short, branching corridor that ends with a flashing red door.

Great! you think. A flashing light usually marks something important. Maybe atmospheric circuits or energy cores. With luck, you could capture one of those systems and teach Lexor and those other two that humans aren't pawns for their war games.

Peering around, you search for signs to identify what's behind the door. Nothing. The door flashes. Red: DO NOT OPEN. It *must* house electronic circuits! Red: DO NOT OPEN. Or even a fusion pack. Red: DO NOT OPEN. You really hate signs telling you what to do!

Open the door on PAGE 72.

Anxious to see, you squirm and twist as the hooks retract into a pressure chamber. You sit still when a gravelly voice behind you orders, "Quit wiggling till I get you outta there! Hmmph . . . space junk! Folks keep litterin' up the universe with trash!"

When heavy cutters separate you from the pilot's seat, you turn and stare into black eyes and a red-brown face. Scrap heaps surround you both. Are you in a space junkyard?

"I'm Hermit," the man says simply, meeting your stare.

Over steamy bowls of tea you tell Hermit about Lexor and Baramus, your science project, and the feud with Fred over his digital point of view.

He shakes his head. "An old story. I prefer it out here with my megacrunch collector where it's pure and calm. Say, you might too! Care to roam the galaxy with me?"

Roaming the galaxy sounds interesting, but you did promise to weed the garden for your mother.

Roam for a while with Hermit on PAGE 33.

Head for home on PAGE 39.

You've seen enough! Time to head for home.

Before Finder guesses your intentions, you leap for the molecular scrambler. Your weight reactivates the molecular action, and in a flash you appear in your backyard. Home again. On good old terra firma, with good old humans!

Suddenly Fred and two others pop up over the fence to stare at you, still standing on the case. You groan. Well, they're not *all* good old humans!

"Hey," Fred taunts. "Leavin' town so you won't be embarrassed when I win the science fair?"

They laugh as you step off the case and pick it up, your bare feet glimmering from the transport ray. Fred appraises your gleaming toes and says, "Neat trick. Takin' up magic instead of science, huh? Why are you walkin' around in your pajamas?"

You shoot Fred a mean look.

Their jeers follow you to the house as you pat the molecular scrambler and grin. Just wait, you think. Wait till Fred sees my *new* science fair project!

THE END

Marlin's fingerglobe bobs in the dark. "Come. You will leave in my secret escape craft in the hangar bay. Baramus will be attacking soon. When he approaches, I'll radio him Lexor's exact position." As he halts abruptly below an airshaft, you collide with him. "However," he continues, "m'Lord won't attack until all *civilians* are removed, so my job right now is to get you out of here." His "civilian" stings like an insult. Marlin boosts you into the airshaft. "This will lead us to the hangar bay without Lexor's guards spotting us."

Finally struggling into the shaft behind you, he hands Bree his globe. "Bree isn't coming?" you ask, feeling a sudden loss.

"He must send a mind-message to his Koorian fleet. They'll join Baramus during the battle." The old man's knee in your back makes you wish for more time with the strange, brave Koorian. "Flibber," he said. It felt like an important word.

Then it hits you. You are going off *alone*! Spying the hangar bay up ahead, you ask, "Did I mention I've never flown a spaceship?"

Marlin says you'll learn on PAGE 40.

Things could be different. Those words flood your mind when you emerge from the ship somewhere near the Miller's Pond Computer Complex. Computer Complex? Where did that come from?

Gone are the birch and pine groves where your family picnicked. Gone, in fact, is everything and everyone you know. Except for good old Fred. Fred, computer king industrialist who owns the complex and has turned your town into a computer factory.

Armed with Hermit's philosophy, you begin a lifelong fight against the Freds in the world. You go down in history as the first space environmentalist, and win the Nobel Peace Prize for your work.

THE END

You listen to the pulse once more to see if you've missed something. Your heart sinks. The sounds are only static reverberations from a competing signal. It was dumb to think you'd pick up anything *this* soon! You climb into bed, feeling foolish as you fall asleep.

The next morning the doorbell wrenches you awake. Who's up this early on a Saturday? Why isn't Mom answering it? The note taped to your headboard explains why. *Went to antique show with Dad. Back at 4:00—Mom.* The bell rings again.

Groggy, you stagger to your upstairs window, peer through the curtains, and look down. A huge golden-skinned man looks up and smiles. His metallic skin shines in the sunlight. Your skin crawls.

A *golden-skinned* man? Then you spy a metal case tucked under his arm. The bell rings again. Are you going to answer it?

If you're lucky, maybe he'll go away on PAGE 34.

Afraid of missing something, you inch closer to Lexor's warship. Unexpectedly, Baramus fires his engines and moves back. Split seconds later, Lexor blasts the space where Baramus had been with energy beams. NO! Lexor's *not* finished . . . he was only playing dead! Baramus must have realized that in the nick of time. Unfortunately, you were not so clever.

Explosive rays scatter through space, hitting you broadside to split the small craft like a walnut shell. Still strapped to the seat, you hurtle through space.

"Help! Somebody!" Your hysterical voice echoes in the pressure-suit helmet. Unable to stop, you join chunks of debris that spin end over end into nothingness. In the next moment, your chin flops against your chest and your eyelids slide shut.

Sometime later a thudding *ka-whonk* wakes you with a jolt. Too muddled to think, you can only stare as gigantic magnets snake from a grimy ship to scoop up you and your broken craft. It isn't possible! Can it be? Have you been rescued . . . way out *here*?

Turn to PAGE 15.

Awaiting the final attack, your mind floods with images of home—of school, of Flibber. *Flibber?!* Where did *that* thought come from? Is Bree calling you telepathically?

"Flibber. Fire your retroboost engine," comes Bree's voice in your head. You do as Bree says. Your crippled ship limps out of danger as Bree's Koorian space jet swoops down on your attackers and finishes them off with three quick laser blasts.

"Flibber. Follow me to Koor," Bree urges gently. "Our work is done. Baramus is here. He will stop Lexor."

"But I *can't* leave!" you explode. "Lexor's after Earth next!" Then a colossal starship passes over you. Emitting violet rays, like feelers, it bears down on Lexor's ship. You know it must be Baramus's Octedron flagship.

Bree's right, you decide. Baramus will defeat that nasty knight without you *or* the Koorians. Then again, Lexor doesn't play by the rules. Maybe you *should* persuade Bree and the Koorians to stick around, just in case.

You don't see how you could help. Fly to Koor on PAGE 83.

Convince Bree and the Koorians to stay and fight on PAGE 49.

Even if Zetans aren't human, you're too curious to back out now. However, you don't know what they want with you. "What does an EC do?" you ask Finder.

"Do?" He pauses. "Why nothing, except have fun." Finder explains more while guiding you to your quarters. "The Search Council will talk with you . . . and make tests, of course."

You are asking about the nature of those tests when Finder nudges you through a door.

Wait! Don't go in that room before you look around on PAGE 84.

Fear overrules caution and you gather strength to blast through the light cylinder. Free of its force, you tumble on the floor. But when you land, Frank's hisses become mournful yowls. You look up as the cylindrical beam moves to the left, capturing the pitiful cat instead of you. Dumbfounded, you see his body dissolve into electrified particles.

"That was nearly me!" you gasp as Frank's ears disappear. Immediately you switch off your radio gear, hoping somehow that will bring the cat back again. It doesn't.

When panic dissipates, you reflect on the loss of old Frank N. Stein, who had slept on your bed for twelve years.

Sleeping fitfully, you rise at dawn for a solitary walk around the yard, but freeze as you pass the mulberry hedge. Was that a "meow" you heard?

Sharpen your ears and turn to PAGE 46.

In the time it takes to turn back, you are discovered and surrounded by the crowd. "Make way, children!" a sharp voice calls out. A wrinkled lady steps forward.

"Come along, luv," she addresses you. "Our ship's due and Sister Sky must check your name on the boarding list or you can't go to Saturn."

Did she say *Saturn*? "*What* ship? Who *are* you people?" Every head swivels in your direction. Sister Sky speaks.

"Three hundred years ago a Saturnian ship crashed here, stranding our forefathers. Tonight a rescue ship arrives."

Spaceship arriving on PAGE 26.

Stunned, you stare at faces around you. "But you look like . . . like *regular* people!"

"We're humans. Only from one of Saturn's moons instead of Earth." Sister Sky pauses, arching an eyebrow. "And you could be a threat to us, *if* the authorities find out!"

"Who's gonna tell? *Me?* Nobody'd believe *this!*"

Suddenly a joyful shout rises and everyone scrambles for trunks and boxes. Your hair is blown back and a sound like a million wings beating fills the air. Next thing you know, you are shielding your eyes from a blinding white light as a huge craft hovers inches above the field. Your jaw drops open in astonishment. Without warning, three loading ramps snake to the ground and people clamor toward them. For the moment you are left alone.

A trip to Saturn's moons! Every astronomer's dream! Quickly you glance around and spot a pile of packing crates to be loaded. You edge toward the biggest one. Maybe you could slip inside.

This is your chance! Stow away in the box on PAGE 55.

Calming yourself, you adjust the dial until it lines up with a glowing green "Z." Then, one by one, you blot out external sounds: the scritchety purr of Frank N. Stein, your cat, asleep on the receiver; the whir of recording tape; the *thump ka-thump* of your heartbeat.

You tremble with excitement as you hear a hum growing inside the receiver. Oddly fuzzy-headed, you feel charged air particles surround you. But before you can think, streaks of colored light swoop into the room from out of nowhere. Blue fluorescent light hits your window and ricochets off your desk. The light bounces up to the ceiling, then down to the floor, leaving a trail of blue behind it. Red, yellow, and green streamers of color zoom around the room in all directions. Finally the colors come together to form a tube of rainbow light. You are trapped inside the blazing cylinder. You look out at your cat, back arched, hair standing on end. His paws seem glued to the radio box.

Frank's panicky hissing triggers your own panic. Run, break free, your emotions dictate. Your mind, however, warns *that* could be a fatal move!

Run with your emotions on PAGE 24.
Freeze on PAGE 75.

For days you work at adjusting to Koor. And with empathetic Bree nearby, you begin to appreciate the primitive beauty of this place. Your time is spent simply: in meditation; in learning the deadly, though rarely-used, hand-fighting techniques all Koorian youngsters know; in also learning that "Flibber" means giving up a part of yourself.

The Koorian philosophy of generosity plus tolerance balanced by strength swells your spirit, but you also realize that the Koorians gain from your native skills. A boldness and willingness to test ideas, so typical of Earthlings, lets you discover fresh uses for Koorian resources—like the molecular gum you develop for repairing everything from tools to wagons to spaceships.

Your spaceship . . . ready now to take you home. That is, if you still want to go. No longer are you only a citizen of Earth. You belong to Koor, too.

No one said the choices would be easy. Go to PAGE 81.

The ship rises high, preparing for a time jump. You glance back at shrinking Koor, wondering if things on Earth have changed as much as you've changed since you were first whisked into space. You smile at Bree, who is focusing on the job ahead.

All at once the ship is tossed and hammered by swirling particles. "Magnetic spacestorm!" Bree yells. Terrified, you grip the arms of your seat and nervously chew your lip.

Your ship is tossed to PAGE 9.

Smiling, you approach the group and ask, "Where's everybody going?"

Your smile dies when a short man whips around, pins your arms, and yells, "Intruder!" As if on signal, the scowling man plows toward you, hands reaching for your head.

"Gently, luv," the old lady cautions, following him. "Earthlings react oddly to memory blocks."

Terrified, you are aware only of fingers gripping your temples. Just before you black out you hear something about "returning home to Saturn."

Terror returns later when a flashlight floods your eyes. "What're you doing here?" a Miller's Pond ranger demands.

Sighing, you say, "I don't know!" At last recollection, you were hearing weird music over your receiver at home. "I was sleepwalking?" you suggest to the policeman.

After a ride home in his patrol car, you sit at the receiver again. A message — "0100 . . . Miller's Pond" — plays beneath the recorded music while a name, *Saturn*, tugs at your mind. Somehow there's a connection. Why can't you remember?

THE END

Sticking with Marlin, you gasp as the beam blasts you through time-space. "Ouch!" Marlin hollers as you both hit your bedroom floor. Before you can quiet him, your parents rush in and stare as breaking sunlight glints on your rainbow-charged bodies. All day you try persuading them that Marlin is *really* from space and *really* has no place to go. He helps by calling them "Gentle Sir" and "Kind Lady." Prior to bed that night you check your science fair project. Marlin asks why you look so miserable. Handing him your project plan, you say, "It's a dud."

Next morning, however, you awaken to find Marlin hunched over your desk. Before your unbelieving eyes stands a model of Lexor's warship, complete with hangar bay and blinking navigational lights.

"I'm glad I could put these plans I stole from Lexor to some use." Marlin smiles. "It's just like Lexor's ship in every detail," he says as the tiny ship rises and hovers above the table.

"This is the greatest science project in the world — in the whole universe!" you shout. "*Thanks*, Marlin!"

Marlin shrugs, but you see his eyes twinkle as he replies, "It was nothing . . . all in a knight's work!"

THE END

The corridor is inky dark. Three yards into the blackness you slide your hands along the rough walls for guidance, steadily creeping forward.

"I'll find a way outta here," you say doubtfully, trying to reassure yourself. Then you freeze.

In the pitch-black hallway ahead you sense a presence. Something waits . . . lurks just inches away. You cringe at a rustling near your hand.

"Who . . . who . . ." you are stuttering when a hand yanks you through an opening in the wall. In less than a second, another hand clamps over your mouth.

You are in deep space trouble! Can things get worse? Find out on PAGE 53.

As your attachment for the solemn man grows, roaming for "a while" becomes years. With quiet dignity you float the cosmos, ridding every star system of trash.

You think about home, and when broken-down freighters stop at the junkyard for parts, you ask, "How's Earth?"

Then one day a long-haul cargomaster looks at you with real surprise. "Haven't you heard? They sent up too many fusion satellites. A couple bumped into each other. Earth's a pulsar now."

You mourn for your planet, but the Hermit reminds you that at least the history of Earth is preserved through you. Years later, when he dies, you mourn again. But you continue wandering, to finish the job he started. And now, you are called The Hermit.

THE END

You flatten against the wall, then hear the front door open.

"Peek-a-boo. I see you!" the man croons.

Does this clown think you're a *baby*? And what's the idea walking into people's houses uninvited! You storm downstairs, but cool off when you see him standing on the porch, smiling. He hasn't come inside.

"What's this peek-a-boo stuff?" you demand.

His smile fades. "Isn't that right? My species book said young humans liked that game." Species book? About *humans*?

Go on to PAGE 35.

"Allow me to introduce myself. Finder at your service," he says, sweeping past you. Then he mutters, "Data on primitive planets is so limited!"

Primitive! You start to protest — until you see him up close. He has no hair, no eyebrows. His eyes are like green pools of water. And stranger yet, even in the dim hall, his skin glows.

Unbothered by your stare, he says, "When you are through scanning me, we will go."

"Go where?" you ask, puzzled.

"To my spaceship and Zeta 12, of course." He cradles the metal case. "My molecular energy scrambler and reassembler's all warmed up, and we *must* return before the Search Council adjourns." His brow ridges wrinkle. "But I got your signal, so you already *know* that!"

Did Finder come because of your space message? Maybe, but it seems he's confused you with someone else. You're not willing to point out his mistake, however, and miss the chance for a ride into space.

All aboard for Zeta 12 on PAGE 93.

"Help me? How?" you ask, waiting for their story.

The old man grumbles, "By dispatching you from this ship before you cause more trouble!"

"*Me* cause trouble? Listen Mr. . . . Mr. . . . ." You fumble for a name to call him.

He straightens. "Marlin the Mentor, trusted adviser to m'Lord Baramus, true leader of the Octedron." Prompted by an impatient purr from the creature, Marlin adds, "And Bree, here, is from the planet Koor. He is our star system's greatest space navigator. That scoundrel Lexor abducted us from Baramus's fleetship!"

You peer into Bree's opaline eyes and say, "Then you've been kidnapped, too."

Marlin nods. "With Bree to guide him, Lexor can rule the galaxy and never be stopped. He thinks we've come over to his side, but even now we are working to thwart his deadly plan." A warning in Marlin's gray eyes chills your blood. "Next on Lexor's schedule," he says flatly, "is your planet."

You shudder. "What can I do?"

Marlin tells you on PAGE 17.

It's time to go home, you decide, heading for the men in silver. You yell over the dock's clamor, "Hey, officer! I need some help!"

They listen as you explain about your radio beacon and following Finder to his spaceship. The tallest man levels amber eyes at you. "Finder! From Zeta 12?"

You swallow a sudden uneasy feeling. "You know him?"

"Sure!" The man grabs your arm. "The Zetan comes through every year lookin' for pets to give to his Search Council. But you're the first one to escape."

"He must have jumped into Finder's package transport," says the other man.

You are pulled along, numbly realizing you were right about Finder. Too bad you were wrong about the men in uniform.

A vivid memory of your aunt Sylvia's large, perfumed poodle with pink toenails and a rhinestone collar follows you into your holding cell. "Pet!" you say glumly. "Well, when Finder gets here to claim me, there's one thing he'd better get straight. No one's putting a rhinestone collar on me!"

THE END

You take your place with Baramus and the Koorian fleet. You fly for several hours until Lexor's dark warship looms into view.

The inspiring telepathic song of the Koorians fades to a whisper. You hear a command in your head. *Flibber, you stay here. Draw Lexor's fire.* To your surprise, you see the entire Koorian fleet peel off and follow Bree into the blackness of space. Wait a minute! Where did they go? Is this some joke? It's just you and Baramus against Lexor.

Before you can question further, Lexor's ship lets loose its first laser blast. Tiny drone ships fly out from Lexor's ship. *Pow!* You fly right into the laser fire of a drone ship.

Suddenly, from over the top of Lexor's ship, come the courageous Koorians. A sneak rear attack! It works. The drones are unprepared for the overwhelming Koorian fleet. Bree himself swoops down in time to save you from Lexor's drone. You nurse your crippled ship under Baramus's protective wing and watch as the Koorians down the drones one by one. When the last drone is gone, Baramus levels the final blast at Lexor. The evil ship pulsates and then blows into pieces. Victory for Baramus! Safety for Earth.

Earth. Will you ever see it again?

Turn to PAGE 89.

You are anxious to get back to Earth, but warily eye the tin-can craft Hermit offers as your vehicle home. "No faith in my system?" he chides. "I made it myself out of space junk."

You regret leaving this sage veteran of three galactic wars, but you are eager to see Earth again. Finally wedged into the ship, he reminds you that the time relefactor gauge is acting up. "You may not land back in the same time zone you left," he warns. "Keep a sharp eye on it, or things could be different when you get back."

See if anything on Earth has changed on PAGE 18.

Crawling out of the airshaft, you find yourself at the door to the hangar bay. Marlin fishes in a trunk and pulls out a silvery pressure suit. "Step in. I'm attaching this cable to your suit," explains Marlin. "It will shoot you over to my craft." He picks up a piece of headgear and holds it next to your head for fit. "I'll maintain radio contact with you through the headphones in here."

Marlin gently pushes you through the hangar door pressure lock. Before you stand spacecraft of every description.

Suddenly the cable attached to your suit is energized, and soon you are being shot through space, feet kicking in all directions. Your ride ends abruptly when you smack into a small red craft.

You push up the hatch and, unlocking the cable, you climb inside. Marlin's voice crackles through the headset. "The remote is all set for Earth."

You study the controls. One lever is pushed forward in a slot marked AUTOMATIC. Beside it is another slot marked MANUAL. Maybe you *should* leave the fighting to experts. Maybe not.

Set the controls to MANUAL on PAGE 69 and join the fight.

Leave the ship on AUTOMATIC on PAGE 90 and head for home.

You step back from the chamber as Finder reaches your side. He pats his heaving chest. "Oh my! That chamber . . . you would've been . . ." Shortness of breath keeps him from finishing the sentence, but he faces you with a sad, green-eyed gaze. "Are *all* Earthlings like you?" he asks.

You flush defensively. "Like what?"

Finder shrugs. "So troublesome! I've offered you adventure, companionship, and what do I get?" His irritated words trail off and he spins abruptly on golden feet, striding back to the main chamber. You follow.

"I'm taking you back," he announces flatly. "Somewhere they must list data on a more suitable subject!"

Data. List. More suitable subject. A silly grin spreads across your face as you hurry along at his heels. You can think of a *perfect* subject for a trip to Zeta 12!

Your "perfect" suggestion appears on PAGE 4.

Instead of a landing-mode, the lined button activates the high-speed override. You and the tiny ship plunge to Koor faster than ever. As the ground rushes up, you squeeze your eyes shut against the impact.

When you open them again, however, you are lying on a stretcher under an apricot sky. "Where . . . how'd I get down?" Three-fingered hands stroke your hair and Bree's thought-words fill your fuzzy head.

"These Flibbers, your helpmates, used mind-suspension to slow your craft. We are home."

As much as you care for Bree, Koor could never be your home. "I want to go back to Earth," you say quietly.

Bree calls out when your words die. He gestures to your spacecraft, smashed into two halves in a nearby field. "Stay, Flibber," Bree says aloud. "Your ship is beyond repair, Flibber."

Accept Koor as your new home on PAGE 66.

Keep trying to get back to Earth on PAGE 80.

You shove Krill aside and bolt for the door. His taunts follow you down the hall until you turn a corner. Halting to get your bearings, you look around, seeing nothing but an eerie chamber several yards ahead. Colored swirls of light coming from inside the chamber make you shiver, but you race for it anyway when Finder sweeps into view, hollering at you.

"Wait! Don't go in . . . stop! It's dangerous!"

He sounds panicked, and you wonder why. Is he only afraid of loosing his EC? Or is he really concerned for your safety?

It takes just a moment to decide.

If you think he only cares about a human subject for the council's study, climb in the chamber on PAGE 5.

He hasn't harmed you yet. Decide not to enter the chamber on PAGE 41.

Forgetting your own safety, you race to the warship, maneuvering onto the hangar bay. Smoking wreckage surrounds Marlin, who lies unconscious near a yawning hole in the bulkhead. You jump from the craft and speed to him. Grabbing his wrist, you feel for a pulse—he's alive.

You strain to lift him, but even though the old man is thin, his bulky spacesuit makes him awkward.

Finally exhausted, you rest, unsure now if you can ever haul him into your small ship. You've had some first-aid training, but don't know if it will help Marlin now. You also fear there may not be time enough to revive him before the ship blows.

Try to haul Marlin aboard your craft on PAGE 64.

Try to revive him first on PAGE 7.

Quickly you scramble under bushes to find a limp, but fully reassembled cat. In the following days, however, you realize a different Frank has returned to you. This Frank runs, leaps, chases, and hunts like a kitten. Whoever captured him in that beam was able to make his aging body young again. Incredible! you think each time Frank streaks up the oak trees.

So incredible that Frank changes your life. You become an astral-biochemist, and with your cat's help, search for the secret of youth, hidden with someone, somewhere in the stars.

THE END

You search your memory for first-aid treatments you learned in school. *Cover the victim to help prevent shock.* You race for an old trunk, hoping first-aid works for space creatures, too.

"Help?" he mutters as you cover him. Moments later, he sits up, unhurt. His downy fingers grip your wrists and he repeats, "Help." Now the word sounds like a sigh. Suddenly you realize *help* is the only word he knows.

Through sign language you learn that his ship homed onto your signal, but a second ship tracked him and should rescue him soon. You *also* learn he is clumsy, when he skids down the stairs and *you* skin a knee breaking his fall.

In the next hours he bounces off, wriggles under and leaps from everything in the house. You bump your shins, turn an ankle, and scrape both elbows trying to stop him. Finally exhausted, you struggle to your room, thinking, "That rescue ship! It *mustn't* get lost!"

Quickly you switch your radio gear from RECEIVE to SEND, then your fingers press the keys. The transmitter hums urgently as over and over you beam out a new message: CALLING OUTER SPACE. HELP!

THE END

"I have to fight! The fate of Earth depends on it!" you bravely tell Baramus.

"We fight, too," volunteers Bree. "Koorians are Flibbers with Baramus. Flibbers with Earth, too." Bree then seems to go into a deep trance. A lilting purr hums through your mind. You hear the message he is sending telepathically to all Koorians: *Flibbers in danger.*

The next thing that happens shocks and thrills you. From every domed habitat on the Koorian hillsides, from every pasture, from over the mountains, come Koorians of all description. The old and the young, male and female, all come toward the center of the Koorian city where you and Baramus stand. In your head you hear a beautiful, inspiring song. The Koorians are all singing in unison. You hear their song in your mind, not with your ears.

Bree leads the crowd of Koorians to a large warehouse with sliding doors. The crowd helps him slide open the doors. Inside stands an army of small, sturdy-looking spacecraft for as far as you can see. You see Marlin's silver and red craft in there, as well. Your space gum worked wonders! Marlin's ship looks as good as new.

The Koorians enter the warehouse and each Koorian climbs into a ship. Wait until Lexor sees this army of Koorians!

Prepare to face Lexor on PAGE 38.

"Stay, Bree," you plead. "Baramus *needs* us!"

If you stay, I stay too, Flibber, Bree replies telepathically. He rejoins the squad preparing to launch a new attack. A half-mile away, Lexor's fighters circle his warship like drones protecting the queen bee. You wriggle deep into the pilot's seat, impatiently rev up emergency engines, and wait to launch with the Koorian.

But before you can begin, Baramus unleashes a huge laser bolt at Lexor's fleet. The blast blinds you. When it fades, you count only wisps of smoke where Lexor's fighters were.

In silent awe you see the evil knight's crippled warship pulse ominously, futilely trying to limp beyond Baramus's firing range. Then the pulsing dies, and Lexor's ship is trapped, waiting to be finished off. You count the seconds, wondering why Baramus doesn't put an end to Lexor's quest for tyranny.

He *must* have a reason for holding off. Can he see something you don't see?

Hang back and wait with Baramus on PAGE 13.
Go in for a closer look on PAGE 20.

Heart thumping, you gape through your windshield to see three of Lexor's fighter jets approaching. They close, photon torpedoes aimed at your craft. You bank steeply as one gunship fires.

Then, luring one gunship close, you fire your own series of laser ram rockets. They all miss. Frantic now, you open up again, three, four times. You don't hit a thing as other fighters surround you.

Your spirit breaks as you are pitched and tossed by a violent blow. With control gauges winking, the ship shudders to a halt. You've been hit!

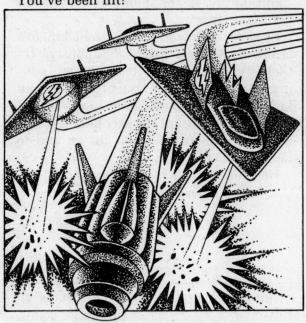

Don't quit! Turn to PAGE 21.

The night is still as you turn up a gravel road to Miller's Pond and enter the park. Beyond a grove of birches, you make out a distant crowd, lit by fires ringing an empty field. Funny time for a cookout, you think.

The crowd gazes longingly at the sky, their voices raised in song. That's the same off-key tune you picked up on your receiver! Only they've added words you don't understand.

"Oh well," you whisper over a rumbling stomach. "A cookout means food in *any* language."

It's not until you've nearly reached the first group of people that you notice stacks of suitcases and trunks; see a tiny old lady in pink leading the song; spy the scowling man protecting her. Maybe it's a tour group . . . leaving after a midnight supper? In any case, you suspect this is no ordinary cookout.

If you sense danger, get out of there fast! Turn to PAGE 25.

If you are curious enough to ask where they're going, turn to PAGE 30.

Your head swims in confusion. You feel split by two loyalties. Help Baramus and Koor? Or go back to Earth? Fight with Baramus now? Or warn Earth about Lexor? Koor? Earth? Koor? It's too much for you to handle and your mind short-circuits from the strain.

Unaware that you've grown rigid and are staring straight ahead, all you hear is a soft, faraway purr as Bree tells Baramus, "A culture clash, m'Lord. It's happened to others, and being alone in a simple environment always cures them."

Let's hope it cures you, too, on PAGE 57.

Strong arms loosen when you stop struggling. Weak from fright, you turn and see the old man. "Hush!" he warns, a fingerglobe lighting his face. "The two of us are here to help."

You recognize him immediately. "I shoved you when I ran from the control room," you say.

He arches a white eyebrow and rubs one hip. "Indeed!"

You gasp when a shimmery creature with misty eyes and a blowfish mouth enters the circle of light.

"Don't be afraid of Bree," the old man assures you. "We're working together."

The scientist in you studies the creature covered with iridescent scales. It reminds you of a trout in Miller's Pond. The rest of you recoils as it extends a three-fingered hand to stroke your hair. "Flibber," it purrs.

Flibber? You back away. Who needs help, anyway! Then again, it's a big cold spaceship out there!

Slip away from the creature and old man on PAGE 14.

Ask about their offer of help on PAGE 36.

You'll need help to get off this ship alive. And that old man looks wisely cool-headed. You'll insist he make Lexor find a peaceful way to solve his problem.

Before the knight reacts, you stride to the old man and yank one dusty sleeve. "Lexor's threatening my planet. You've got to talk him out of it!" Your demand is followed by Lexor's laughter.

The old man shrugs. "See how much influence *I* have? I'm a prisoner, young one. Like you."

Your mouth falls open as Lexor approaches, aiming a silver ray gun at your chest. "The difference, Marlin, is that I'll turn *this* one into a *fighter* with my mind-enslaver gun."

"No chance!" you argue as an icy blast suspends your emotions and your body. Then from the corridor you hear the thumping of booted feet marching to a chant: "Le-xor! Le-xor!" Iciness melts and you race to fall in behind the last fighter. "Le-xor!" you chant. What a *wonderful* sound . . . you'd follow it anywhere!

THE END

You squeeze inside the crate just in time to be hoisted onto the ship by an electronic lift. The crate hits the cargo bay floor as electronic engines rev up, but you sense no liftoff or speed until G-forces press you against the inside of the crate. Then the bay is heavy with silence. The silence of deep space?

A floating sensation answers your question. Weightlessness! Pushing up the crate's lid, you instantly sail like a helium balloon toward the ceiling. One panicky lunge for a passing pulley sets you aspin, bouncing off bulkheads, slamming into crates.

"Ouch! Ooof!" Each stop is punctuated with a protest. Moments later your "flight" ends. You crash to the floor in a rain of barrels and crates and lie there for several seconds, panting.

"It looked like fun when the *astronauts* did it!" you mutter, rubbing sore spots.

Bruises heal quickly in space. Turn to PAGE 56.

Feet planted again, you wonder who or what switched on the gravity. You spy a porthole across the cargo bay. In your haste to look through the round window, you stumble over a crate. Its contents rattle across the floor, but no one seems to hear.

Finally you peer out the porthole and your breath stops. Suspended below is a familiar blue-white sphere, halved by darkness. Above the dark rim a gleaming orb stands guard over sleeping planet Earth. Awestruck, you almost don't react when the bay door swings open.

Silhouetted against the light, a man roars, "Who's in here?"

Well, you have two choices.

Tell the truth and hope for the best on PAGE 87.

In this jumble of boxes he won't see you. Hide on PAGE 78.

By the time Bree ferries you from Koor to a rest camp on a tiny orbiting asteroid, your whirling mind is clearer. "But I *can't* stay here! What about Baramus? What about Earth?" you protest when Bree explains.

"You must stay, Flibber. The Earthling in you is fighting the Koorian you've become. Only time will tell you which is stronger. You need time alone to think."

As Bree and his ship lift off again, you look around at your simple shelter and the rocky hills. You thought fighting with Fred back home was bad. And fighting Lexor out here in space was worse. Now you've started a fight with yourself! That's the worst of all.

You slump to the ground and pull your knees up under your chin. It looks like you lost *those* battles. You hope you can win *this* one!

THE END

When you press the button with wavy lines, outer space reverses. Suddenly everything looks like a photographic negative. Time reverses, too, stars become black streaks moving backward through the sky. In the swirling mass, Bree has disappeared. So has the planet Koor. You cling to the seat of your craft and wait for the tumult to subside.

Tingling from the toes up, you feel a familiar panic. The tingling sweeps upward. Your whole body feels as if it is breaking into electrified particles.

Your body crashes onto a hard surface, and you hear a voice say, "Excellent! The Macron Transporter beam is working again."

He's there! Just as before! Lexor looms over you, explaining about Baramus and his own "noble quest." You activated a time warp instead of the landing-mode! Filled with dread, you realize that you have traveled back through time. You are right back on Lexor's ship.

You yank away from the knight's poking and sputter, "That's enough! Now tell me where I am and what's going on here!"

Funny. A moment ago you thought you knew.

PAGE 76 will refresh your memory.

Your craft skims closely along the warship's hull. You try ignoring blast reflections from the ongoing battle that illuminate the cockpit. In seconds the hangar bay looms ahead and you drop into hover-mode to locate the panel.

It's there you note with a sinking stomach that Marlin mentioned only one red panel, not two!

Another flash of laser light draws your eyes spaceward as a trio of wasp-fighters dives at you. Spotted now, you grope for the rocket trigger. Hurry! You've just one chance to pick the correct panel!

Destroy the left panel on PAGE 85.
Blast the right panel on PAGE 68.

You don't think Earth's leaders will react very well to threats. Besides, if there's a war, you might be the first casualty!

The sound of clanging metal makes you jump. In that instant, the knight's attention is diverted to a hunched old man, poised in the open doorway across the room.

Think fast! Escaping through that door might be your last chance! All right, not much of a chance. Where could you go? Maybe the old man is more reasonable than Lexor. You could talk to *him* about a solution that doesn't involve war.

Dive through the doorway on PAGE 10.
Reason with the old man on PAGE 54.

Creeping from the shadows, you look around the space station, hoping for an idea of what to do next. Your spirits soar at the sight of two silver-uniformed men wearing shiny badges. Space police!

As you peek around the far side of *Saturnian Spacecraft One*, you see an unused ramp flanked by people-sized boxes. You could stow away!

The two men in silver head for the darkened ramp. Quick, decide what to do!

Take a ride on the SS1 . . . PAGE 55.
Ask the men for help on PAGE 37.

"I'm pretty good at video games," you tell the boastful robot.

"I wanna play!" Krill toots, zooming around chairs and under a hammock.

You walk over to one of the video games. Lifelike holographic men play a game that looks like lacrosse. You hit the buttons, but it doesn't affect the game at all. This is no fun.

Finally, disgusted, you walk to the door muttering, "Forget it! I'm finding a new room."

The robot freezes. "No!" he beeps. A glass door slides across the doorway, locking you both in. At the same moment the video screens go black and disappear. They were just holographic images! When they are gone, all that is left is a room with glass walls. You gasp. In the next room and the next, are other extra-celestials, each with their own version of Krill. Different creatures, you realize, from different galaxies. Finder's a zookeeper, not a scientist!

You sink into the swing as Krill announces, "I am your companion, forever." Then he bumps you annoyingly. Krill could even make you appreciate Fred.

THE END

You grab Marlin again as the ship tilts, suddenly dropping several feet. You fall. Scrabbling for a foothold, you slide to the craft, dragging along Marlin's limp body. You both stop at the craft's landing shanks. With dread you realize Lexor's ship is breaking up . . . *now!*

Braced in the craft's hatchway, you clutch the cowl on Marlin's spacesuit. After a giant heave, his body slides inside and you jump over him, ram the craft in high gear, and race for space.

The contest ends seconds short of safety. An intense internal force rips Lexor's ship apart, hurtling your craft through space, and you into unconsciousness.

Is this it? The end of everything? Find out on PAGE 92.

"Maybe exercise will help keep me awake," you sigh. After a quick jog around the room, you jiggle the knob on the receiver. Your hand freezes. An off-key melody drifts from the set. Weird! No radio station broadcasts this far down the dial.

As the tune repeats, you hear words, numbers too . . . don't you? ". . . er's Pond." There it is again. "0100. Miller's Pond."

You glance at your watch. Hey! That's military talk for 1:00 A.M., thirty minutes from now. You run to your closet to get a sweater. With your arm in one sleeve, you stop to think. It's late, you admit sensibly. Should you be wandering around Miller's Pond at this time of night? What if this is just some late-night talk show DJ playing a joke?

If you think Miller's Pond is worth investigating, turn to PAGE 51.

If you think it's just a radio contest run by Late-Night Floyd, the DJ, turn to PAGE 91.

The impact of Bree's words overcome you. Earth images — Disneyland, Miller's Pond, your parents, and your cat — familiar visions fill the warm air. But gentle Koorian hands help you control the lump in your throat, and in time you become aware of your new surroundings.

Take a look around Koor on PAGE 67.

With Bree at your side, you explore the Koorian countryside. Far off, a dwarf blue sun throws gray shadows on simple domed homes set in the soft hills. In the valleys you see herds of animals resembling long-necked goats.

As time passes you grieve less for your old life and begin introducing new ideas to the Koorians. You teach them how to hold elections. You do away with the previous method of selecting a leader — picking the Koorian with the shiniest fins. Working with the gentle Koorians teaches you the *real* meaning of "Flibber": helping . . . sharing all that you are and know . . . being a true friend.

Years later, when Lord Baramus and his galactic knights visit Koor again, they find that you have been elected governor. Although busy and content on Koor, sometimes at night you climb a hill and search the starry skies for that distant blue-water planet called home.

THE END

The rocket blows out the right panel with a blast. Reeling from the shock, you regain control and prepare to dodge your attackers. Clammy-cold, you search for them, wondering if you've completed the mission successfully.

Strange, the trio of fighters stalking you has disappeared. Stranger still, as you scan the battle zone, you see that swarms of Lexor's fighters have become silly, directionless bees, flying in circles.

Suddenly you realize you *did* hit the communications panel . . . and *more!* Unknowingly, you also disarmed the knight's drones — pilotless drones he must have directed by remote control with a ship-to-ship system.

"Marlin! Bree! We did it . . . we stopped Lexor!" you shout into the headset as Baramus fires a last photon torpedo at Lexor's warship.

Your pounding heart stops when it explodes. Does Baramus know that Marlin is still trapped in the ship? Instantly your craft is aimed for Lexor's hangar bay. You *won't* let Marlin share Lexor's fate.

Go get him on PAGE 45.

The future of Earth is at stake. You're not going to be packed up and sent home like a baby! You are ready to fight! You yank the lever back, locking it in MANUAL. Suddenly the ship trembles and spins. In terror you remember that you don't have any idea how to fly this thing.

"Civilians *never* follow orders!" the old man sputters over your headphones. "Push the steering stick. Fire the counterthrust engines!" he barks as you spy a padded stick by your knee.

Gentle it forward. Easy! With perfect timing, fusion engines fire front and left, stabilizing the craft. Still gulping air, but flushed with confidence, you test the steering, while a display board tracks you like a video game. Tingling with excitement, you emerge from a sloppy spiral to notice something is missing.

No vertigo. No sickening sense of falling or being squashed by G-forces. You yell into the helmet microphone, "Hey Marlin! I can fly!"

His reply is marked by alarms that scream through the cockpit. WARNING flashes across the display board as three waspish fighter planes show up as blips on the screen. Their blips are chasing your blip!

It's time to fly . . . or die on PAGE 50.

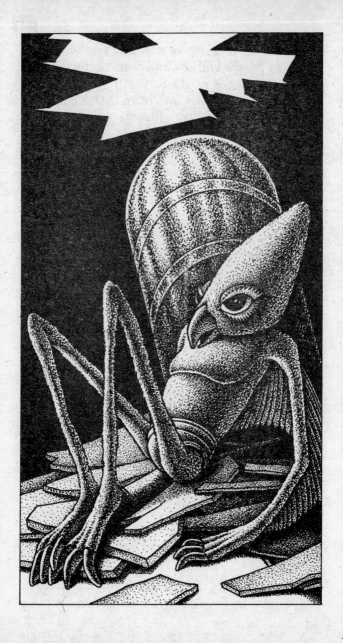

Snuggling into bed, you listen for the swish of recording tape and yawn. Since your parents are leaving early for an antique show, you can sleep late.

Next morning, a crash rockets you from bed. Flat-voiced moans drift from above your head and in moments you are up the stairs, bursting through the attic door. Sunlight fills a hole in the roof. Mere confusion turns to fright when you spy a four-foot-long charred cylinder poking from beneath a heap of rubble.

Incredulous, you creep around the cylinder and gasp. Sprawled beside it is a birdlike creature, with spidery limbs, covered from top to bottom with dove-gray down.

Slowly it flutters golden eyelashes to reveal pleading, frightened fawn eyes. Then a tiny mouth whispers, "Help!"

Great Galaxy! It sounds like the voice from the radio last night. What'll you do *now*?

Try first-aid on PAGE 47.

You open the door. When the crack widens, you glimpse a small, dark chamber beyond. Watching the passage for Lexor and the old man, you shoulder through the door. It shuts once you are inside.

You look around, then your heart stops. Directly overhead a panel lights: GARBAGE EJECT CYCLE ON. Oh no! You're in the trash chamber, being dumped into space!

Slowly a hole opens into empty freezing blackness. You wish you didn't know what was coming.

As the yawning hole widens, an unrelenting vacuum pulls you closer . . . closer. A strange vision forms in your head. You picture a huge monument. It has been built to honor you . . . the first casualty in Earth's war with the alien Lexor.

It looks like you are finally going to be first at something. How come you feel like a loser?

THE END

Cramped in Marlin's small craft, you can't tell how long or how far you've traveled. You *do* know the ship has passed three time tucks, where space miles pleat and are spanned in moments. You can tell when you're in a time tuck because planets and stars zoom past at incredible speed. Soon you enter Earth's solar system.

Silent with wonder at piercing the solar windshield, you cling to reality. But it's hard to react scientifically to the beauty of tiny Pluto hung like an ice crystal. It's hard to contain your emotions as the craft skims milky blue Neptune crowned with two moons.

Then Jupiter crowds out everything else. White, red, brown bands shroud the hulking world that watches space with a dusty red eye. Over its rim you glimpse Gannymede and Callisto, large Jupiterian moons. Suddenly a third object rises. You recognize the square mirrored panels of Nomad II, the orbiting telescope launched from Earth years ago. You laugh at the contrast between manmade and celestial creations. The sights imprint on your memory in vivid detail.

Turn to PAGE 74.

Nearing Earth, several time tucks later, your craft turns, presenting its heat shield to the atmosphere. You faint just before the tiny ship plummets like a burning stone into a foothill lake.

Before long, you struggle ashore, leaving behind the only evidence of your trip. You can't imagine what you'll tell your parents.

In years to follow you become the world's foremost space artist. "Amazing," critics say of your work. "Almost as if you've really been out there!"

You smile and say, "Yes. It *is* amazing!"

THE END

You feel your toes tingle, then the tingling sweeps upward. Your whole body feels as if it is breaking into electrified particles. Moments later you slam onto a hard vibrating surface.

"Excellent! The Macron Transporter beam is working again. I had hoped for *something* useful, but an Earthling, how wonderful!"

An excited voice snaps your eyes open and you stare at a bearded man in a tunic emblazoned with a badge. Your head crowds with questions, but you can only stammer, "How'd I get here?"

"On a macron beam. Everyone knows if you shoot macrons around space long enough, you'll hook *some* kind of creature." He shrugs, then pokes your arms. "But the thing has been malfunctioning and I feared it might capture only half of you." He jabs you again and announces, "Fortunately for me, you're all here."

"Fortunately for *you?*" You yank free, sputtering angrily, "Now what's going on here?"

Go to PAGE 76.

The man bows stiffly. "I am Sir Lexor, Knight of the Octedron Order and Governor of Koor." Cottony fear smothers you as he adds, "And you'll stay here until you help us."

Before you can object, Lexor slumps in a chair. "Lord Baramus has driven my knights and me from our planet, and now he's trying to drive us from our galaxy." His voice hardens. "Look at my fleet!"

You follow his finger to a viewport. Strung out like a tattered kite tail are black spaceships linked by laser cables.

"Earth shall be my stronghold, a haven for repairing my ships!" His dark eyes narrow. "Instruct your leaders that we come in peace. They'll listen to one of their own."

Impulsively you blurt out, "Fat chance! Who listens to kids!"

Lexor's face reddens with fury. "Truly, that complicates matters, but you *will* convince them. Otherwise, it's war."

You're not too crazy about this guy. First he kidnaps you, then orders you around. *Now* he's spouting about war!

Turn to PAGE 61.

Again and again the fighters pound Baramus's flagship while the Koorians streak in to draw their fire. You are left behind, feeling useless and nearly weaponless, with just one remaining laser rocket. Even Bree has joined the fray. Isn't there some way you can help?

A bold thought races through your mind. Maybe one ship could inflict damage on Lexor's warship. But how?

Almost immediately your headset crackles. It's Marlin! You can barely hear his raspy voice beneath the static. Has he been trying to contact you all along? That must be it. Energy from the laser weapons has been jamming the frequency. Suddenly you slip beneath the warship's belly and his message clears.

"Knock out the red communication panel! The one just below the hangar bay . . . and don't waste any more time!"

"On the way, Marlin!" you yell into the microphone.

You're back in action on PAGE 60.

Crouched behind overturned metal barrels, you try to hide until a spotlight sweeps across the cargo bay. The man's attention is drawn away as someone joins him, and you scramble inside an empty barrel, leaving the top ajar to hear their words.

"Look at all this junk! I *told* them we were taking too much," the man grumbles.

A second adds, "What can we do?"

Then a solid kick rolls your barrel across the deck, activating the barrel's automatic vacuum-pressure lid. Just before the cover clamps shut you catch a final phase.

". . . jettison these barrels into space."

Go for an unexpected ride on PAGE 88.

Following Marlin by seconds, you squeeze onto the Macron Beam Transporter platform, bracing yourself against the wall to stay upright. Marlin sets Earth coordinates on a blinking directional guide and yells, "Here we go!"

He activates the beam producer. It chugs, coughs, and wheezes while your toes tingle and pulse. *Wait a minute!* A terrible thought enters your mind. Lexor said this thing was malfunctioning ... remember?

Desperately, you glance back at the hangar bay. The craft is still intact. Should you stake your life on a faulty Macron Beam Transporter?

Stay put and hope Marlin knows best on PAGE 31.

Jump off and try your spacecraft instead on PAGE 8.

You yank away from the Koorians and scramble for the injured craft. "I can fix it!" you tell Bree, trying to fit the halves together. Then you turn to the other Koorians. "And if *they* could bring us down here safely, they can get me home again. They *have* to!"

Bree's eyes cloud. His strong voice repeats, "Flibbers!" He points out each creature lying on the ground or leaning against the outcroppings.

Now you focus on them. Their chests heave and their bodies are covered with dark, bruised patches. They are hurt . . . really hurt! Your panic changes to gratitude when you realize how much they've sacrificed. They may have even risked their lives to ease you through the perils of deep space. Doing it again could kill them.

"I'll stay," you tell Bree.

His sad purr matches the tone of your voice.

Turn to PAGE 28.

Yet another choice is presented to you a week later when Baramus arrives. As his flagship lands, you know something's wrong. The Octedron ship is pocked with scars. A dignified but war-weary Baramus rushes to you. "YOU! You're the *last* hope of the galaxy. Come quickly or we're lost!"

Stunned, you ask Baramus what's happened.

The warrior rests and tells his tale. After you and the Koorians left him battling Lexor (and winning), the evil knight unleashed waves of drone fighters he'd hidden in space. Baramus's starship barely escaped. Since then Baramus has been running, and now Lexor is preparing to attack Earth.

"I know, *somehow*, you are the key! If you hadn't gone, things would be different," Baramus says. "Go back with me!"

Your head reels. If Earth's at stake, you should get home and warn *them*! Still, Baramus seems sure your presence with him will turn the tide.

Go with Baramus on PAGE 48.

Return to Earth and tell them about Lexor on PAGE 82.

You can't decide. Think about it more on PAGE 52.

"You're just guessing that my being there will make a difference, right?" you ask Baramus. He nods. "Well *I* don't have to guess! If I go back to Earth I can convince people to rally forces and *whip* Lexor there!"

Baramus studies you and says, "Then you must try."

You watch as the Octedron flagship disappears through cloud layers accompanied by Koorian fighters who've agreed to help Baramus. Faithful Bree remains, choosing instead to go with you.

You try persuading him to stay on Koor. "Look, Bree. I can make it alone if you just pre-set the navigation guide." But deep inside you want Bree to come, although you're not sure that's best. How will Earthlings react to the scaly little Koorian?

Bree shakes his head and continues loading supplies into the craft. "No," he insists. "Space sectors between here and Earth are too unpredictable. I'm going."

Aim the spaceship toward Earth and hope for the best on PAGE 29.

"I'll come, Bree," you say.

Bree explains that if you relax and allow contact, his neurons can lock onto yours. Then by controlling your hands he will bring both ships safely to Koor.

"Relax? Control my hands?" How can you relax at a time like this! "Look, Bree, if it were anyone but you ..." Your protest spent, you drift into a lazy sleep state, aware of soft purring in your mind.

Time seems to have stopped when you are jolted awake again by the bouncing ship. "Hey! What is this?" Your foggy mind clears enough for you to see you've entered Koor's atmosphere and are plunging toward the surface.

"Relax, Flibber! You've broken contact with my neurons," comes Bree's urgent whisper.

Unable to relax, you search for the landing controls and shout feverishly, "I'm gonna crash!" Wait. Those two square buttons might activate the landing-mode.

Choose button on PAGE 58.

Choose button on PAGE 43.

Wide-eyed, you stare at a room alive with blinking video games and flashing holographic images of Earth. Finder rushes out the doorway. "I'll send in Krill for playtime . . . right away!" he calls back.

Playtime? Krill? His words make sense when a spheroid robot glides into the room waving spidery, jointed arms. "Bet you can't beat me!" he beeps rudely.

You stare. That's *it!* This Krill character reminds you too much of Fred. Maybe you should find a way off this crazy ship.

Run for it on PAGE 44.
Stay awhile on PAGE 63.

You squeeze the rocket release mechanism and feel a surge of exhilaration as the left panel shatters. Bracing for attack from the wasp fighters, you arc your craft sharply and glance spaceward. Puzzled, you see them peel off, accelerating rapidly *away* from you.

A moment ago they closed in as if you were helpless prey. What's happened?

Suddenly the tearing, twisting eye of an invisible vortex closes in on you instead, sucking you through the blast hole in Lexor's ship . . . down, down into the terrifying recesses of his fusion engines.

With quick, painful insight you know what's happened!

What? What? Turn to PAGE 86 and find out.

The left panel was *not* a communications core, but a fusion fuel intake valve, feeding matter into a hydrogen converter. You've read articles about thermonuclear fusion, but on Earth no one's made it work. Despairingly, you note that Lexor's scientists are smarter than Earth scientists.

As the fierce whirlwind drags you ever closer to the engine's center, one last thought flashes through your mind. "Marlin, you muddled old fool, you really blew it!"

But, you have to admit, you're the one who is going to get a blast out of this adventure.

Ka-boom!

THE END

"It's me! I'm a stowaway," you confess. "I only wanted to see Saturn, honest!" You tremble as you watch the man approach.

"A stowaway," he mutters. "And an Earthling, too," he adds. "Looks like we're stuck with you," he says.

Great! you think. You are really going to visit Saturn!

"You'll have to be isolated for a while," says the man. "Some native Earthlings carry germs that can be fatal to our planet."

Your grin disappears. Isolation doesn't sound like fun. Then you recall that Earth's astronauts were isolated for two weeks when they returned from space. It's worth two weeks alone to see the ringed planet.

You follow the man to a chamber in a distant wing of the ship. The Spartan room offers little comfort, but you have a view of space from a tiny porthole.

"Exactly how long do I have to stay here?" you ask the man.

"Not long," he answers, pushing a button that seals the room. Through a speaker his voice crackles, "We'll be able to tell if you're not a disease carrier in about one hundred and fifty years."

What!? One hundred and fifty years! You stagger backward to the metal bunk bed. You won't bother to ask how long it will take if you *are* a carrier.

THE END

88

Without further warning, you are shot into an endless void. Trapped in the pressurized barrel, you see nothing, hear nothing. The claustrophobic blackness makes you gasp, turning shallow breath to icy moisture that slides down the barrel walls. Only a sick rolling in your stomach tells you the barrel is spinning.

All at once your stomach quiets. The metal cylinder seems frozen in mid-spin, suspending your legs over your head. An instant later, fresh panic grips you! A brilliant rainbow-colored beam fills the barrel. Your toes start to tingle.

Someone is really scraping the bottom of the barrel this time! Discover who on PAGE 75.

You're glad Earth is safe, but sad to think you'll never see it again. If there was ever a chance of going home, it's gone now. Your small vessel is crippled beyond repair.

Later, when you are aboard Baramus's ship, you can't seem to join the revelry. "What's the matter, my friend?" asks Baramus. "We've won a great victory today."

You explain that you want to go home more than anything in the universe.

"I think I can work a little wizardry in that department," comes a familiar voice.

"Marlin! You're alive!"

"Beamed aboard just before the blast. I've been thinking about you," he says. "Baramus can fly to the edge of this solar system, and I think that we can safely beam you home from that distance. Anywhere in particular you would like to land?"

You think about it for a minute and then whisper into Marlin's ear. "Very good," he chuckles.

Back on Earth, Fred is proudly walking up to receive his first-place ribbon in the science fair—when suddenly a sparkling cylinder of light forms in the center of the stage! Slowly a hazy figure begins to appear within the light. The figure steps forward . . . it's you! The judges call a recess to reconsider the awards. You told Fred you'd find a way to win first prize.

THE END

Your hand hovers over the lever, but you leave it set in AUTOMATIC. Still shaky from your cable ride, you ask Marlin how he'll escape Lexor, since you have his craft.

Marlin grumbles. "Never mind! Baramus'll beam me on the flagship before he blows Lexor's fleet. Now you watch the navi-guide! Keep that craft on the Earth channel." His voice softens and fades as fusion engines launch you into space.

Speeding away, you look back as a squad of Koorians arrive to batter drone fighters from Lexor's warship. Dizzy from the spectacle, you almost miss Baramus's approaching starship. Without warning, it looses a blast that suddenly illuminates the blackness of space. And when the blast dies, Lexor's fleet is gone. Awestruck, you realize that Baramus has saved unsuspecting Earth.

Nerves steadier, you turn to the glowing navi-guide marking your path home. Good. It looks easy to handle.

Follow the navi-guide to PAGE 73.

You like radio contests, but don't care for Floyd's style. You snap the receiver off. You sleep so soundly you don't see the glowing spaceship rise from Miller's Pond and hover outside your window, don't see it climb into space.

Next morning your mother hands you a newspaper article. "UFO AT MILLER'S POND?" the headline reads.

Three days later at school, the science fair winner is announced. Your report about picking up strange signals and then missing the UFO that might have sent them takes first place. But who cares! You lost the chance of a lifetime. If you had followed the signals, you might have been on that ship instead of just writing about it!

THE END

Marlin's voice rouses you from unconsciousness some time later. "Young friend! Thank goodness you're alive!" he exclaims, shaking your shoulder.

"Quiet, good Marlin," comes a deep, soothing voice. You look up from the bed on which you are lying to see a tall, silver-haired man with kind, brown eyes.

"Save your strength," says Baramus to Marlin. "Bree reported your plight before he returned to Koor. Our tractor beam brought you both aboard.

"You'll be macron-beamed home," Baramus assures you. "But first, brave deeds must be rewarded. Kneel there," he orders, lifting a sword handle from which projects a shimmering laser light. Baramus's laser sword buzzes you gently on each shoulder. "I dub thee liege of the Octedron Order. Rise and be known forevermore as the Knight of the Star-Spangled Scanner!"

You rise, feeling proud, but you can hardly believe it when Baramus hands you his laser sword. "Take this sword," he says, "as a symbol of your knighthood."

You look at the sword with awe. You came a long way in your search for the perfect science fair entry—but Fred will have to go a long way to beat this science project.

THE END

Wow! A trip to Zeta 12! Okay, so Finder is a little odd. He *seems* harmless. And you can always ask about this Search Council stuff later.

Adjusting his metal case, Finder explains that it holds a portable transport ray. He pulls you onto the humming case and clutches your arm. An instant later, you are aboard a sleek, futuristic spaceship.

The molecular transport scrambler still hums when Finder settles it near his feet to study you. He claps his hands. "A *fine* extra-celestial sample for the conference! Now skeptics *must* believe there's life in this galaxy."

"You mean I'm *your* extra-terrestrial?"

"Extra-celestial," he corrects. "And I'm very glad I found a *human* subject this year."

You gulp.

Did you act rashly by coming with Finder?

Grab the molecular scrambler and beam home on PAGE 16.

You are an open-minded scientist. Be Finder's EC on PAGE 23.

Collect All the Twistaplot® Books